I Can Read!

SHARED
My First
READING

Biscuit
Wants to Play

WITHDRAWN

story by ALYSSA SATIN CAPUCILLI
pictures by PAT SCHORIES

HarperCollins*Publishers*

HarperCollins®, 📖®, and I Can Read Book® are trademarks of HarperCollins Publishers.

Biscuit Wants to Play Text copyright © 2001 by Alyssa Satin Capucilli Illustrations copyright © 2001 by Pat Schories All rights reserved. No part of this book may be used or reproduced in any manner whatsoever without written permission except in the case of brief quotations embodied in critical articles and reviews. Manufactured in China. For information address HarperCollins Children's Books, a division of HarperCollins Publishers, 195 Broadway, New York, NY 10007. www.harpercollinschildrens.com

Library of Congress Cataloging-in-Publication Data

Capucilli, Alyssa Satin

  Biscuit wants to play / story by Alyssa Satin Capucilli ; pictures by Pat Schories.

    p.   cm. — (My first I can read book)

  Summary: The puppy Biscuit makes friends with two kittens.

  ISBN-10: 0-06-028069-7 (trade bdg.) — ISBN-13: 978-0-06-028069-7 (trade bdg.)

  ISBN-10: 0-06-028070-0 (lib. bdg.) — ISBN-13: 978-0-06-028070-3 (lib. bdg.)

  ISBN-10: 0-06-444315-9 (pbk.) — ISBN-13: 978-0-06-444315-9 (pbk.)

  [1. Dogs—Fiction. 2. Cats—Fiction. 3. Play—Fiction. 4. Animals—Infancy—Fiction.] I. Schories, Pat, ill. II. Title. III. Series.

PZ7.C179 Bit 2001   00-027154

[E]—dc21   CIP

                                                                                                               AC

16 17 18 SCP 20 19

❖

For Peter, Laura, and Billy
with love
—A.S.C.

Woof, woof!

What's in the basket,

Biscuit?

Meow.

It's Daisy!

Meow. Meow.

Daisy has two kittens.

Woof, woof!
Biscuit wants to play
with the kittens.

Meow. Meow.

The kittens want to play

with a leaf.

Woof, woof!

Biscuit wants to play, too.

Woof!

Biscuit sees his ball.

Meow. Meow.

The kittens see a cricket.

Woof, woof!

Biscuit wants to play, too!

Meow. Meow.

The kittens see a butterfly.

Meow. Meow.

The kittens run.

The kittens jump.

Meow! Meow!
The kittens are stuck
in the tree!

Woof!
Biscuit sees
the kittens.

Woof, woof, woof!

Biscuit can help the kittens!

Woof, woof!

Biscuit wants to play

with the kittens.

Meow! Meow!
The kittens want to play
with Biscuit, too!